Calling ALL CaRS

written by
Sue Fliess

illustrated by
Sarah Beise

sourcebooks
jabberwocky

Adobe Photoshop was used to prepare the full-color art.

Published by Sourcebooks Jabberwocky, an imprint of Sourcebooks, Inc.
P.O. Box 4410, Naperville, Illinois 60567-4410
(630) 961-3900
Fax: (630) 961-2168
www.sourcebooks.com

Library of Congress Cataloging-in-Publication data is on file with the publisher.
Source of Production: Leo Paper, Heshan City, Guangdong Province, China
Date of Production: December 2015
Run Number: 5004858

Printed and bound in China.
LEO 10 9 8 7 6 5 4 3 2 1

For my Madsters and Little "A"
—Sarah

For Kevin, thanks for being my
road trip partner for life
—Sue

Big cars,

small **cars,**

Beach cars,
town cars,

tops-go-down cars.

Zip through tunnels.
Make no stops.

Climb up over mountaintops.

Long cars,
WIDE cars,

who's inside cars?

Smash cars,
ram cars,

DEMOLITION
DERBY

BEEP!

traffic jam cars.

Yellow taxis,
limousines,

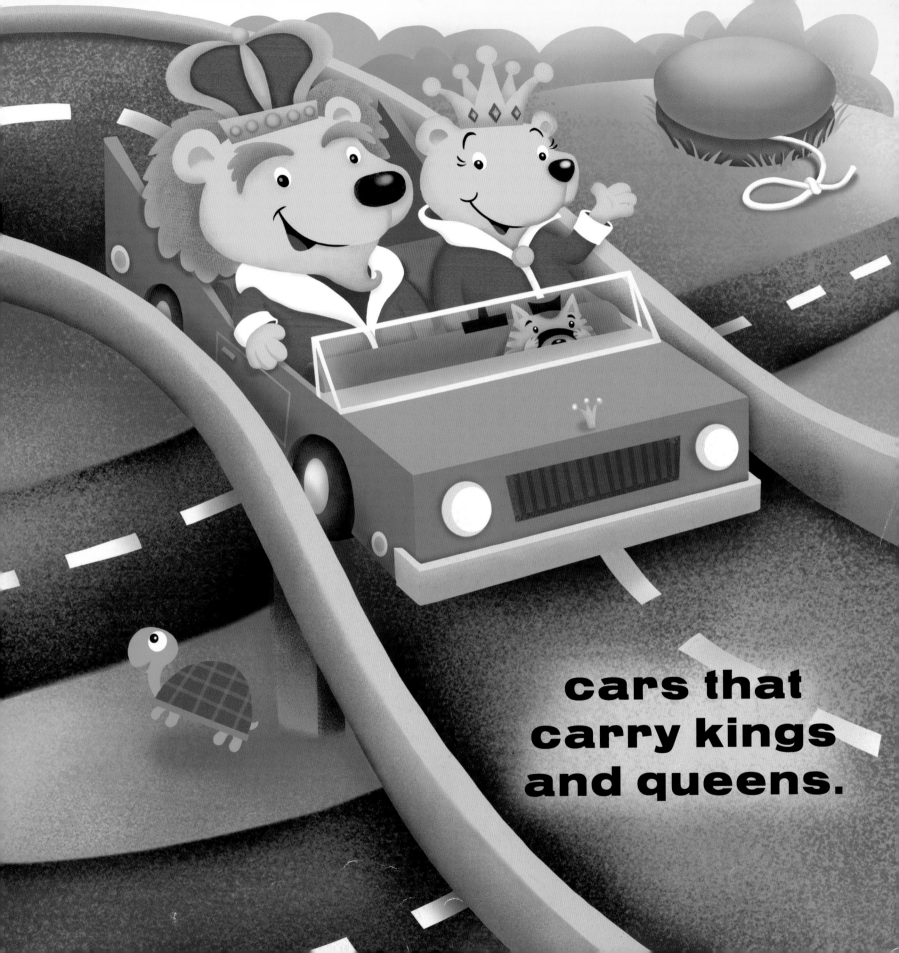

cars that
carry kings
and queens.

Up
cars,

down
cars,

circus-clown cars

Fast cars,

slow cars,

way-down-low cars.

Honking horns and changing lanes.

Ice and snow?
Let's put on chains!

Trip cars,

track cars,

dogs-in-back cars.

**Old cars,
new cars,**

starry-view
cars.

Rest, cars.

Hush, cars.

CAMP

No more
rush, cars.

Cars pull in,

turn

off

the

light.

Sweet dreams,
sleepy cars...

good night!